The
Sheep Follow

For Lydia,
Dawn, and Clarity

Library of Congress Cataloging-in-Publication Data
Wellington, Monica.
The sheep follow / by Monica Wellington.
p. cm.
Summary: Frolicking sheep follow various animals as they go by and
then are too tired to follow their shepherd.
ISBN 0-525-44837-3
[1. Sheep—Fiction. 2. Animals—Fiction.] I. Title.
PZ7.W4576Sh 1992
[E]—dc20   91-3420 CIP AC
Published in the United States by Dutton Children's Books,
a division of Penguin Books USA Inc.
Designer: Carol McDougall
Printed in Hong Kong by South China Printing Co.
First Edition   10 9 8 7 6 5 4 3 2 1

The artwork is done in gouache on paper
with details in color pencil.

The
Sheep Follow

Monica Wellington

DUTTON CHILDREN'S BOOKS   NEW YORK

The shepherd leads the way.
And the sheep follow.

Look—a butterfly!

And the sheep follow.

The geese waddle in a line.

And the sheep follow.

The cat walks along the fence.

And the sheep follow.

The pigs get into the corn.

And the sheep follow.

The rabbits run to the woods.

And the sheep follow.

Fish swim past.

Some ducks paddle by.

And the sheep follow.

The dog barks.

He chases the sheep—

right back to their shepherd.

The shepherd is ready to go.
But the sheep won't follow.